MY PHSYCO STALKER

AF551238

AUTHOR K

Copyright © Author K
All Rights Reserved.

ISBN 979-888521650-0

This book has been published with all efforts taken to make the material error-free after the consent of the author. However, the author and the publisher do not assume and hereby disclaim any liability to any party for any loss, damage, or disruption caused by errors or omissions, whether such errors or omissions result from negligence, accident, or any other cause.

While every effort has been made to avoid any mistake or omission, this publication is being sold on the condition and understanding that neither the author nor the publishers or printers would be liable in any manner to any person by reason of any mistake or omission in this publication or for any action taken or omitted to be taken or advice rendered or accepted on the basis of this work. For any defect in printing or binding the publishers will be liable only to replace the defective copy by another copy of this work then available.

Contents

Prologue

Hi, I am Ji-ho. You guys are going to read my story. And this is how I look and the people in my story.

This is me Ji ho

This is my bestfriend (Taehyung)

This is my other best friend (Jimin)

This is my other best friend (jungkook)

This is my Oppa (Namjoon)

This is jungkook's cousin little sister (Lisa)

And this is my stalker (Ji-hoon)

CHAPTER ONE

THE STALKER'S ENTRY

It has been seven years ago. When I was 18 years old and was studying in a Korean university. I will be sharing an incident that I will never forget. Whenever I think about that incident, I get cold shivers on my body sometimes I even get depressed. So, Let's start..........

It was 2015 when this incidence took place in my life. I was living with my big brother Kim Namjoon because my parents died in a car accident. Namjoon Oppa (Oppa is a Korean word that means big brother) was just like my mom, dad, and best friend. So, after our parents died me and Namjoon Oppa started living with my aunt Si-Woo. She lived alone because uncle Sung-Ho died on a mission because he was a police officer. After my aunt's death, we shifted to a new city " Seoul" which was also in Korea. After shifting we joined the university in Seoul. Of course!

FIRST DAY OF UNIVERSITY

I was walking after parking my car near the university's gate. Today was my first day and Namjoon Oppa was not with me as he was tired after all the shifting work, I asked him if he needs help but he said no and today he must be sleeping in bed. Anyways I was walking and was finding someone to help me find Mr. Choi's office (Principle). I was thinking until I was three boys talking to each other near the university's gate. I approach one of the boys and said Excuse me, Will you please help me find the way to Mr. Choi's office? (Taehyung's pov: I, Jimin, and jungkook were talking until a random girl approached us and asked in a calm yet confusing way - Excuse me, Will you please help me find the way to Mr. Choi's office? Before I could reply Jungkook said // taehyung's pov ends...) Jungkook said Hiii!!! first of all, I am Jungkook, and what's your name ??? My name is Ji - ho. Nice to meet you, Sorry if you don't mind I am in a hurry...... before Ji - Ho could continue Jimin interrupted in between and said OHH!!!!!! Ji - Ho, namjoon oppa 's small sister RIGHT!!!!!!!!!!!!!!!! Yes, you know namjoon Oppa Ji - Ho said in excitement. Jimin nods in reply. Taehyung said OOhh - ok!! So lets us help you to explore this university. Ji - Ho nods in reply. And all of us left for the university tour

Jimin,Jungkook,Taehyung and Ji - ho

SECOND DAY OF UNIVERSITY

After parking my car near the university's gate again I was walking but today my car was a bit behind from my yesterday's place. UNTIL I felt someone behind me. I turn back to see a new guy he seemed to be lost So, I asked him if he needs help.

Ji - Ho and the new guy

The new guy said shyly Hi, I..... I......I am... Ji....hoon. Ji - Hao said with a wide smile Ohh! My name is Ji - Ho. Isn't our name similar? Ji - Hoon said with a smile OOhh yeah!! Then Jimin,Jungkook,Taehyung came to Ji - Ho.

New member in the group Ji - Hoon

(Ji-Hoon 's pov: After the girl's name my blood boiled but I managed to force a smile. Her name was Ji - Ho, it was okay that it was the same as mine but it was the same same as my twin Ji-Ho. she was my twin 2 years back. I said two years back because, I killed her two years ago and killed her in a way the ait look like she had a suicide attempt, and she passed away. I hate her just can't even take her name like that much. And if I got a choice I could kill her twice or thrice. And look here we got a new whole Ji-Ho.WOW!!! JUST WOWW!! Ji-Hoon 's ov ends)

Ji-Ho: Hey boys!!! how are you guys?

Taehyung: Heyyyy cutie (:

Jimin: Heyyyyy Ji-hooooo O:

Jungkook: Ahhhhh Good morning shorty (;

Taehyung: Who is this dude???

Ji-Ho: Ahhh!! This is my new friend Ji-Hoon.

Jungkook : (hesitantly) ammm......am... isn't .....isn't your name similar?

Ji-hoon: yeah (:

Jimin: Anyway welcome to our friend group.

Ji-Hoon 's face reaction from inside...

GET READY TO DIE JI-HO!!!!!!!

MORE TO READ............

CHAPTER TWO

SOMEONE IS BEHIND ME

Days pass by and the friendship between Ji ho and the boys grew stronger and stronger...........

Here are some lovely moments of the boys and Ji-ho(;

Ji-ho and Ji-hoon

Jungkook and Ji-ho

Taehyung and Ji-ho

Jimin and Ji-ho

Okay, so now let's continue the story................

One month later.......

Ji-ho was walking to her home after her classes as her car wasn't working all her friends knew it even Ji-Hoon knew about it. and decided to follow her. Right now Ji-ho was walking in a dark alley all alone and had headphones in her ears and singing. Ji-hoon was walking behind Ji-ho who was still listening to music. Ji-ho was still 20 minutes away from her house. when her phone got discharged and then Ji-ho thought to keep all the stuff back in the bag. Ji-hoon was about to stab Ji-ho with a knife when suddenly Ji-ho stopped and looked behind because she felt like someone was behind her, but saw no one and continued walking. After a few minutes, it started raining and Ji-ho again felt someone behind her so she looked back when she found ....

Ji-ho turns behind to see.....

TO CONTINUE.........................

CHAPTER THREE

THE HORRIFIC EXPERIENCE

TO SEE THIS....

Ji-hoon standing behind her. Ji-ho first got scared because she couldn't see Ji-hoon's face due to the lighting and saw this.....

This is what see saw........

Ji-ho was scared as hell and the best option she could think of at that time was to run and begin running as fast as she could crying a mess.

Ji-ho while running

After running for a while Ji-ho reached home.

(Ji-ho pov: I was crying a mess and was running as fast as I could. But after a while, I saw my house and saw Namjoon Oppa standing with an umbrella. I saw him and fell to the ground. Ji-ho pov ends)

Ji-ho and NamjoonShe fell down

(Namjoon pov: I was waiting for Ji-ho. It was already 7 PM and the university was already closed at 5 PM and I had called Ji-ho's friends. They said she was not with them and she left for home as soon as her classes were over. I was worried as hell. I don't know what my little sis was suffering through and I didn't want her to suffer more as she had already suffered while childhood. I was thinking this and was going to find her when I saw her crying a mess and fell on the ground I ran to her and pulled her up to stand up. Namjoon pov ends)

As soon Ji-ho got up she hugged namjoon crying.

Ji-ho and NamjoonShe hugged him.

Namjoon says in a worried " Princess, what happened why are you crying?

Ji-ho trics to say while crying " Oppa.......(sniffs)Oppa....... I saw........ s.......s..s.s...some.....someone!!!!!!!

Namjoon says " princess, please stop crying and calm down.....

Before Namjoon could say more Ji-ho passed out. Namjoon quickly picked her up in his arms, took her to her room, laid her down on her bed and covered her with a blanket, and called a doctor..........

TO BE CONTINUED..................

CHAPTER FOUR

My Little Nightmare

After the doctor reaches, he quickly checks Ji-ho and says " Mr. Kim your sister is fine, she just passed out due to fear. I am giving you some medicines give her the pills on time, after 30 minutes she will wake up. Namjoon sighed in relief and begin to wait for Ji-ho to wake up. Then Namjoon went down to cook something for her sister. When Namjoon was cooking he didn't realize how time passed. But, suddenly he heard a scream. As he heard the noise he quickly ran to Ji-ho's room as the noise was coming from her room. As soon as Namjoon reached Ji-ho's room he saw Ji-ho screaming. Namjoon says " PRINCESS, why are you screaming. The sudden shouting of his brother made Ji-ho shut her mouth and flinch a little. Namjoon realized his shouting made his sister scared then he says in a soft voice " princess, sorry to shout at you. But will you tell me why are you screaming? Ji-ho calms down and says Oppa, I saw a bad dream. Namjoon says " what you saw? Ji-ho says"

I ran free at night

sat on the bench in the park enjoying the sight

saw a shadow in the woods looked at it and felt not so good

the shadow was coming closer to me and my soul left my body

the shadow was starring at me I felt like drowning a sea
the ground extends and finally, the nightmare ends.....
(This is a poem written by the author of this story)

Namjoon says: Princess, you know it was a bad dream right?

Ji-ho says : (hesitantly) Yeah...yeah I do.

Namjoon says: then, princess /:

Ji-ho says: But, Oppa I got scared):

Namjoon says: It's okay, princess. now quickly take a bath and come downstairs. (You must be thing did Namjoon Oppa forgot what happened with Ji-ho. No, he did not he just thought not to talk about it as she already was scared due to her dream.)

After coming down they both had their dinner and went to bed.

Ji-ho could not sleep that night. She was lying on her bed and was thinking about the incident before.

Who was that? Ji-ho was thinking.

The next.........

Ji-ho got ready and was leaving for her university but Namjoon said Taehyung will be going with her. Ji-ho agreed and left for university with Taehyung.

Taehyung and Ji-ho walking to the university.

I Almost Died

Taehyung 's pov: Last night I was lying in the bed and was thinking about Ji ho's car because in the morning her car was working perfectly as I asked her if I can use it and of course she agreed after I came back and parked the car. And someone called me it was one of my classmates I was standing a bit far from Ji ho's car I had a little chat it was the new girl Lisa she was junkook's cousin's little sister. When I was coming back to Ji ho's car. I saw Ji hoon was standing near Ji ho's car before I could go to him he wore some kind of hoodie and a mask he looked some type of psycho. Suddenly I got a call from namjoon Hyung (Hyung means brother) He said he want me to walk Ji ho to the university by tomorrow. I was about to speak when I heard Ji ho's voice and Hyung ended the call. I got worried and decided to talk to Ji ho in the morning. Taehyung pov's end)

Present time

In the morning with Ji ho..........

Taehyung: Ji ho......

ji ho : Yes, tae what happend ?

Taehyung: What happened to you last night?

Ji ho suddenly begin trembling in fear and fainted, Looking at Ji ho's condition taehyung picked Ji ho up in his arms and called jimin to pick them to pick up.

Taehyung picked up Ji ho

Jimin arrived and asked Taehyung what happened to Ji ho.

Taehyung: DUDE!!! CAN'T YOU SEE HER CONDITION (In a shouting voice)

Jimin: chill man, I was just worried about her.

Taehyung: STOP TALKING JIMIN.

Jimin: Then keep her in the car.

Taehyung and Jimin sat in the car and they left for their university

IN THE UNIVERSITY.........

As soon as they reach the university Taehyung quickly ran to the university's infirmary still Ji ho was in his arms. Then after a few minutes, Ji ho woke up and was looking at the nurse.

Nurse: Miss Kim, are feeling good?

Ji ho: Yes ma'am, Can you please call who dropped me here?

Nurse: Yeah. Mr. Kim and Mr. Park(Said to Jimin and Taehyung who were waiting outside)

Taehyung and Jimin entered the room.

Taehyung: Hey, Ji ho are you okay?

Jimin: Yeah, Sweetie are you okay?

Ji ho: Yeah, Can you guys take me to the beauty mount but jungkook should also come okay??

Jungkook comes running from nowhere and says

Jungkook: Hey,Ji ho are you okaaaaaaaaaaaaaaaahhhhhhhhhahhhhhhhh......

Everyone burst out laughing and Jimin got jungkook's hand before he could fall.

Ji ho: Yeah kook, I am fine.

Jungkook: Oh sorry I am late.

Ji ho: Yahhhhh!! why are you being sorry?

Jungkook laughed nervously and said Can I call Lisa also?

Everyone said Yes while smiling.
Ji ho: Where is Ji hoon?
Taehyung: He is not here. He went out.
Ji ho: Ohk, let us go

Then they all left for the park........

All went to the park.

In the park........

Lisa: Ji ho noona (noona means sister)
Ji ho: Yahh sweetie

Lisa: Noona, Are you new here just like me??

Ji ho: No Lisa it has been already 1 year and 6 months since I have known them.

after like near 2 or 3 hours Ji ho and Lisa had been talking the boys were standing a bit far from them when jungkook says to Jimin and Taehyung.

Jungkook: See Ji ho guys she seems getting too close to Lisa.

Jimin: Yes (:

Taehyung: Yeah (:

jUNGKOOK!!!!!!!!!!!!!!!!!! Suddenly they heard a shouting

Jungkook looked at the other side to see.........

I ALMOST DIED

TO SEE JI HO FALLING...........

Lisa: OPPA!!!!!!!! SAVE NOONA (Said while shouting and crying at the same time)

Jungkook jumped to save Ji ho but Jimin held his wrist.

Jungkook: LEAVE MY HAND JIMIN!!! SHE WILL DIE (said while shouting and crying)

Jungkook crying

Suddenly Taehyung said GUYS HERE WE HAVE A LAKE DOWN JI HO MUST BE DOWN.

All of them went running down the mountain to see

- 

1. Ji ho drowning in the lake

Jungkook quickly went flying in the water to save her

After he got her out of the water they all went to jungkook's house.

TO BE CONTINUED......................................

Got To See My Biggest Fear

In Jungkook 's house......

After Ji ho woke up

Lisa: Noona, are you okay??

Ji ho: Sweetie, why are you looking so sad I am fine nothing happened (said while hugging her)

Lisa and Ji ho hugging each other

The boys smiled looking at them.

Next day in the university............

Lisa went running to Ji ho and hugged her.

Jungkook came from the back smiling looking at them.

Jungkook: Yah Miss. Kim, why jumped of the mount yesterday?

Ji ho: Yah, I did not jump Lisa was falling so I pulled her to the ground and I slipped and fell in the lake.

Jungkook: Thank you to save her.

Taehyung and Jimin coming said Earth to you guys we are getting late.

All of them chuckled and left for their classes.

After their classes..........

Lisa: Noona can we walk together to home?

Ji ho: Do you want to walk?

Lisa: Yeah, please?

Ji ho: Okay (:

The boys said they will come after 30 minutes as they had extra class.

So Lisa and Ji ho left for their home. Today also it was raining...

Lisa and Ji ho were walking alone.

A few moments later Lisa felt like someone was behind them and turned around to..........

To see Ji hoon with a knife and quickly stabbed Lisa

Ji ho was shocked to see Ji hoon killing Lisa. And ran to see Lisa lying lifeless on the road.

Lisa died

After killing Lisa Ji hoon got scared and ran away.

LISA!!!!!!!!!!!!!!!!!!!

SHOUTED JI HO................

Crying Ji ho

TO BE CONTINUED..

9 798885 216500

Printed by Libri Plureos GmbH in Hamburg,
Germany